NAZAR

a tale of the supernatural

Richard Morley

suspicions and superstitions

For L

*'when he speaks of [her], or when he refers
to her photograph, it is always under the
honourable title of the woman.'*

CONTENTS

20 APRIL 2004, 18:45

Particulars, Universals,

Tim, your upgrade tactic didn't work. So, I'm standing in a sweltering economy departure lounge in my poshest frock and spikes wishing I'd worn my loons and flats.

As I type, TA668 is sulking. The rumour is that she has a poorly engine. When Jim and I embarked on our honeymoon – a lifetime ago – our flight was delayed for the same reason. What are the chances? (Rhetorical exclamation, Stan). Well, she'll be safer for having been overhauled. ('Not necessarily,' I hear Eleanor object.)

The cabin crew seems unconcerned. All except the beauty standing erect as a kore, her eyes on the window that looks over our prospective ride, her fingers twisting the amulet on her tunic, twin to the evil eye decal on TA668's tail.

Will email again if we make it.

I am therefore I think,

Daph

20 APRIL 2004, 21:35

Particulars, Universals,

Haven't been consumed by a fireball yet. But I did have a heart-attack after the lights went out, and we dropped ten thousand feet. (Turbulence?)

At present, I'm dying of boredom. Why? Just before the doors closed, a great lump occupied the aisle seat. The second the wheels retracted, he/she/it nodded off. Try as I might, I couldn't reach my bag o' books in the overhead locker.

The Lump started awake five minutes ago, when we began our descent, and proceeded to cough and sneeze in my direction. No matter how loudly I tut and come-come, it continues to expectorate as if I'm not here.

Oh, well – I always pick up something when I venture abroad – never what I'd like to – and leave feeling in greater need of a holiday than when I arrived.

I am therefore I think,

Daph

20 APRIL 2004, 23:16

Particulars, Universals,

Disembarking down stairs, in heels, I felt like a film star. The Hollywood treatment continued after I slipped through *customs:* two teenagers at a trestle table who appeared not to see me (being ancient – ergo invisible – has its benefits). Outside, a fun-sized Omar Sharif held up a cardboard rectangle bearing my surname (or almost).

The taxi ride to the hotel seemed interminable, but, in fact, lasted forty-three minutes. Had Omar any English, German, Greek or Latin, I would have asked to sit beside him. For company, you understand. I'm old enough to have been his mother. (Odd how no one is dismayed by the thought of consorting with someone old enough to be their sister.)

Twenty minutes later, he lowered his mobile phone, nodded at his windscreen, and grunted. I peered past the amulet swinging from his rear-view mirror. A great white fin pierced the darkness a mile ahead.

Before I could determine what it was, we veered left, onto a dirt road.

An enervating sense of vulnerability overcame me. Three thousand miles from home, I was being led into the wilderness by a stranger with whom I shared no common language. Were he to pull up outside a cave, then, I wouldn't be able to barter for my life. Why should he do such a thing? The crusades, TE Lawrence – Turks have no reason to be kind to us. And he needn't have been motived by history merely. Blighty boasts wards of disinterested lunatics.

Something dashed into the road. Cat? Dog? Goat? I have no idea. Or knowledge of whether it went under our wheels. My heart stopped again, but my driver seemed unconcerned. On top of everything else then, he was a brute.

We turned into a town not so much sleepy as asleep. The only illuminated interior belonged to the butchers. The three haunches hanging in its window constituted a lost Francis Bacon.

We lurched left again, and up a palm-lined boulevard at the end of which the alabaster fin loomed.

'Otel!' Omar said.

A chic but officious receptionist detained me in the lobby for half an hour to apprise me of treks further afield. It wasn't enough that I had been compelled to pay a single-person supplement/ singleton tax; effectively shell-out for someone who wasn't there. Though the only excursion I was interested in was to Bedfordshire, I suspected that graduation to same was dependent upon signing up for something. So, I obliged. (I'll cancel it later.) Delighted, Officious rewarded me with a free pass to something or other, and offered to wake chef to prepare a late supper for me. I patted my belly and pulled a face. She roused the dozing bellhop. I was permitted to retire to my room.

Daph

21 APRIL 2004, 10:41

Particulars, Universals,

I started awake at the sound of hacking: my own. It was too soon for the rhinoviruses gifted me by The Lump to have begun to bite, surely. Dr Superstition diagnosed an allergic reaction to the local flora.

After a tart's bath, I descended to the restaurant. All I could stomach from a breakfast buffet of Homeric proportions was a small bowl of Greek (is that what the natives call it?) yoghurt, and a demitasse of Turkish coffee (pencil shavings steeped in hot water).

A weedy waiter crossed to my table to replenish the latter, and looked me over concernedly. 'English?', he whispered. I glanced about. His fellow staff members were Turkish; the other diners German to a mensch; what to say, then, with all the old enemies before me?

'Shaz!' someone called out. My waiter started, and

hurried away.

In an effort to recover from my ordeal by cattle class, I resolved to spend the morning stretched out on a sun-lounger. After discovering that I had forgotten to reclaim my bag o' books from the overhead locker before disembarking from the plane, I collected the British papers – smut and small print – from the lobby.

It may not be possible to step into the same river twice, but I dipped my toes into the pool three times. Evidently, it's not cost-effective to heat an Olympics-sized facility out of season.

Equanimity couldn't last. I started awake at what I thought was someone calling to me, to discover a teenager – with the legend *Animator* emblazoned across his t-shirt – bent over me. What did he want? For me to join him in a game of crazy golf. I demurred, and made for the beach before the hotel.

I wended my way towards a toddler who appeared to be entirely alone. Upon realising that the translucent object she repeatedly tossed at the waves and snatched up again wasn't a beach ball, I implored her to desist. Giggling, she ignored me. I dashed across to an elderly woman seated on the low brick wall before the hotel. She resisted my polyglot imprecations. I mimed dying by asphyxiation. She continued to look through me, towards her charge. I witnessed the toddler torment the jellyfish one more time, and strolled on.

Daph

21 APRIL 2004, 14:45

Particulars, Universals,

Following a buffet lunch (another heroic spread picked at), I resolved to take advantage of my complimentary pass to what the introductory hoarding boasted, in Times New Roman 98 point, was an original Ottoman hammam built on the site of a Roman thermae – as much to cleanse my stubborn jet-lag as my pores.

The gruesome old bag behind the check-in desk ignored me. So, I flashed my pass, and hurried inside.

I don't believe that Shaz intended to feel me up. He simply lacked the English to convey what he believed I needed to know, and, therefore, felt compelled to frog-march me back to the hoarding. I pretended to read the fine print.

Later, I found a flyer for the facility, and discovered my mistake. Out-of-season, women are permitted to use the hammam after two only.

Why hadn't Gruesome told me as much? Told me anything?

Daph

22 APRIL 2004, 13:29

Particulars, Universals,

Every seat was taken when the dolmus squealed to a halt before the hotel. None of the passengers disembarked. Nevertheless, the driver left no one at the stop. Having resigned myself to standing, I was delighted when a beautiful young man offered me his seat. The concerned look he gave me was disconcerting, but I grinned like Buddha all the way to town.

I toured the clothes market in search of an authentic entari. All I could source was a brand of tat common to sale rails back home. I bought the nearest equivalent anyway (made in China, I just discovered).

Inauthenticity wasn't my only gripe. Last time I was here, hawkers dubbed me *Elizabeth Taylor*. Jim didn't mind. But I do now that they don't flirt with me, call me *mother* (not merely because it's technically inaccurate), and rumble my nationality before I come within haggling distance. And the flies! Why don't they circle anyone else?

I lunched al fresco at a fish restaurant overlooking the peninsula. Its sole customer, I had the peculiar sensation that I was being watched. (Chance would be a fine thing, you say.) It turned out that I was. Not by my waiter (after taking my order, I didn't see him again for half an hour). Hearing a mew, I looked down. A one-eyed moggie crawled along the embankment. I rewarded the lean, white thing with half my main course.

What has happened to my appetite? Must be the sun. More heat; less meat.

Daph

P.S.

Conjecture: The natives don't discern that I'm English on sight.
Rather, they determine – somehow – that I'm not German; then ask if I *speak* English (the lingua franca for every other tourist).

22 APRIL 2004, 15:45

Particulars, Universals,

I made straight for the hammam on my return to base camp. This time, I paused before the check-in desk, and sang a hearty halloo. Gruesome regarded me woundedly. Perhaps she has no English, German, etc. I hurried in, to spite her.

Why so determined? Jim had repeatedly postponed our trip to the Turkish baths last time I was here. On our final day, I resolved that I would visit one no matter what. The young attendant cautioned me that I would lose my tan. I was vain in those days – vainer; so, I backed out, and told Jim that the place had been closed due to technical difficulties. Had he seen through me? Something caused him to laugh uproariously. Anyway, this time I'm dead set on enjoying steam before stain.

I deposited my clothes in the changing room, wrapped a towel about myself, stepped into the clogs provided, and proceeded to the sıcaklık. It was foggier than anticipated. A real pea-souper. The light drizzling through the tiny windows gave the dome the contingent quality of a cloud. Dampened by steam, the sounds – trickling, coughing – emanated from everywhere and nowhere.

Blind, I inched towards the goebektasas, arms extended like Karloff's mummy. I got the measure of the stone with my fingers, and laid on my belly. Immediately, hands pressed my back; the skin on them rough as a shark's. Or were they sporting mittens? In either case, I froze.

I had assumed that the division by gender would apply to tellaks too, but the fingers were strong, and the grunts of exertion deep. My discomfort soon faded. Vanity, too. I buried my face in my towel, and spread.

Guess what, kids: first tooth-ring to last tooth – ping! – and we're all the same again. All unashamed again.

Daph

23 APRIL 2004, 14:12

Particulars, Universals,

I could say that the reason I joined the tour that Officious had pressed on me was because it was too late to cancel. The truth is that I was tired. (Jet-lag, still?)

Nevertheless, I had intended to jump ship once we reached the site. However, our guide – a local classics student – proved to be so bright, charming and handsome that I was drawn along after we crossed the threshold.

Exhausted, I remained seated after the others exited the amphitheatre. And, for a minute or so, was alone in the auditorium. Oddly discomfiting, the experience brought Nietzsche to mind: *if you gaze long into an abyss, the abyss also gazes into you.* What was it: the ghosts of history? Perhaps, but my money is on last night's dolmados. (I recalled Jim's proscription re. cooled rice too late.)

Unable to locate my party, I determined to head back alone. Having left the site via the rear entrance, I started up the road with the assuredness of someone who has no idea where they are going. Twenty minutes later, it occurred to me that not one dolmus had passed. Or any other vehicle for that matter. Perhaps this wasn't a public road?

Just when I had resolved to turn back, a figure in mufti climbed out of the ditch on the opposite side of the road, turned my way, and waved. Suspecting that ignoring him would invite hostility, I reciprocated. He started across. I looked up the road; down. There was no one – nothing – on either horizon.

Mufti stopped before me, looked me over as much as at me, and said, 'English?'.

Irish, Scottish, Welsh – I have a claim to all three, but didn't think that he would mark the distinction, or judge any of them less culpable for Sykes-Picot. So, I nodded.

He bared strong, white teeth. 'Attaturk,' he said, 'he take idea from -' Frowning, he looked past me.

I determined not to present my back to him. Hearing a shriek, I jumped out of my skin. The dolmus crunched to a stop. Mufti extended a hand. I climbed in, paid the driver, and took the seat directly behind his. Still grinning, Mufti boarded, and proceeded to the back of the vehicle, without paying.

All right, my theory is dead in the water. So, how do the locals always guess my nationality? Maybe it's the simple fact that I'm out here on my own. Freya Stark, Gertrude Bell, all the orientalists – Old bags wandering the mystic East is a peculiarly British affair.

Last time, I got the impression that they didn't like us much. Why should they do so now? The only reason I could come up with is that most – all – of the other tourists are German; so, I'm a rare bird. Exotic.

They want me to be English. Very well, I'll be one hundred per cent, St. George's-flag-knickers English.

Daph

23 APRIL 2004, 18:45

Particulars, Universals,

I shouted greetings at Gruesome today. Her response? She coughed into her hand, and drew her entari tighter. Perhaps she's deaf.

In the caldarium, I dreamt that Jim was gesturing for me to join him in the hotel pool, a come-on-in-the-water's-lovely look on his face.

I started awake from this on hearing someone call to me: 'Prof!'

This had been Jim's pet name for me. I can't recall him ever having used it when we were in public, or me having told anyone what it was, till now.

I felt for my specs. They weren't about my neck, and would have been useless if they had been.

The call went up again.

'Hello?' I said, and squinted into the fog.

Who else would have known that the appellation *Prof* was appropriate? I didn't insist on it when I booked. Then, all of our biographies are at the end of a mouse tail now, aren't they?

Perhaps it was someone's idea of a practical joke. The put-upon Shaz having fun? Or Gruesome?

Often, context is all that separates comedy from cruelty. The locals seem friendly, but probably don't like me – us – as much as they pretend to.

Yes – That explains why they look at me the way that they do.

Daph

23 APRIL 2004, 20:52

Particulars, Universals,

Of an evening, the hotel lobby serves as an ersatz agora. Guests too fagged out to hike into Kuşadası, or leery to stroll the beach in the dark, promenade the marble thoroughfare.

The semblance to a town square is reinforced by the parade of shops along the back wall: an understocked but overpriced souvenir store (authentic Turkish Delight and the like), a boutique showcasing locally-produced ceramics (every item decorated with the evil orb), another offering textiles (more eyeballs), and an internet café (install myself before a VDU on holiday? I'd sooner die). None are patronised sufficiently to justify their existence. Those who venture into them do as I did: glance at the price labels, and wander out again.

No sooner had I settled into one of the settees that dot the walkway than I was accosted. An anxious young woman looked me over as an arborist might an ash riddled with dieback, and bid me join the group on the couch behind her.

Her family? The resemblance was startling. As if the men and women were products of cloning, not sexual reproduction. All save the Goth on the extreme left, a spindly ghost at the feast.

I turned back, and declined in High German.

Evidently relieved, the young woman shrugged, and retired. Someone waylaid her before she reached her seat. He looked nothing like the others. Healthily obese in the way that only Germans can be, someone must have persuaded him that his best hope of acceptance in the world of average-sized folk lay in passing himself off as Santa Claus. How else to explain the white beard and ruby-coloured suit? He peered over her shoulder, and bared his teeth as if he intended to eat me.

Deciding that he was the family's minder, I raised my glass to his charges. Inside, I seethed.

Why do people always assume that those on their own are lonely? That life is more valuable – only validated – when experienced in prides?

Daph

24 APRIL 2004, 14:15

Particulars, Universals,

I rose at dawn, with rosy fingers. My panic didn't abate after I slipped on my specs. Where had the blood come from? I dashed across to the dressing table. A clown leered at me from the mirror.

Having intended to frequent the bar to ferret out the prankster from the hammam, I had returned to my room after dinner last night for a nap. I have never nodded off in full slap before. Evidently, on top of everything else, I have started to suck my thumb. The Seven Ages.

Today's excursion was a jolly affair. Not least because tour guide Maria had a command of the requisite languages such that she could joke in all five. It helped that the operator responded to the modest sign-up by dispatching a mini-bus rather than a coach. This bound us together. As did the fact that, other than the driver, there were no men in our party. (That's how sexist comments may be redeemed, Tim: as anthropological observations.)

I tied the scarf that Maria had supplied about my lustrous locks, and removed my shoes. Before I could follow the others into the mosque, I started; must have done. In any case, Maria took my hands, and drew me in. I told her that I had been overcome by the beauty of the interior. That wasn't true. It had been due to the man standing before the pillar opposite. He looked like Mufti. No – Not *like* him; he was him, surely.

Lunch in the gardens of a hillside restaurant was presaged with an unnerving experiment in interactive theatre. After we had ordered drinks, a cohort of young men in white smocks descended on us, brandishing rapiers. I clutched my heart. It was only after they came within slashing distance that I realised which victims the skewers were intended for. I pointed to one tipped with the silhouette of a lamb. My waiter regarded me – well – the way everyone does here, and turned towards the kitchen.

Daph

24 APRIL 2004, 15:45

Particulars, Universals,

Coffee downed, we returned to the mini-bus, and continued up the hill.

A hundred yards from the summit, the driver cut the engine, and jumped from the vehicle. Had he been caught short? A moment later it occurred to me that we were still moving forward, albeit at a stroll, as if invisible hands were pushing the minibus. A magnetic hill! The driver waved as we passed him. Maria yelped 'Witchcraft!', and crossed herself. The others groaned. The driver jogged after us, and leapt through the door. It had all been an optical illusion, Maria explained. Or as Heraclitus might have put it: the way up was, in fact, the way down.

We turned off the main road, and descended to a traditional carpet centre; more nineteenth-century hamlet than Axminster warehouse. Young women – children – tied each knot by hand (it's the little fingers, apparently). All had remained unchanged since the time of Mehmet. Almost all.

We were ushered into a windowless room, and offered refreshment. I declined the ubiquitous apple tea, and regretted the decision almost immediately. A young man as thin as a Giacometti strode in, and shut the door. Did I hear the lock click or imagine it? I glanced about, searching for Maria. Gabbling in German, Giacometti crossed to a knee-high pile of carpets in the centre of the room, and began whipping one after the other away with the brio of a magician drawing silk handkerchiefs from a jacket cuff.

Twenty minutes later, it occurred to me that our freedom might be dependent on someone making a purchase. The finer examples of child labour commanded thousands. I regarded my fellow captives. All had claimed to be on package holidays too. How likely was it, then, that any of them had a spare grand knocking about? I looked right, along the row of strangers already seated when we entered. They were better dressed than us, yes, but were any of them millionaires?

The stack of carpets was nearly exhausted. So, my hypothesis was about to be tested. After palming the final mat, Giacometti looked over his shoulder, towards the hundreds of rolled carpets at the other end of the room. He wasn't going to unfurl them too, surely?

He pushed himself up, crossed to the door, and drew

it open. Motivated by relief, our applause was wildly enthusiastic.

Daph

24 APRIL 2004, 18:45

Particulars, Universals,

I stopped before Gruesome today, and waved at her for what seemed like a minute. Blind – She must be blind.

Inside, I was awoken from that dream about Jim in the pool by a prick. (Titter ye not!) I rubbed my nose. The mosquito had flown.

'Prof?'

I pushed myself up, and peered into the fog till my elbows went to sleep. Then, I climbed down from the goebektasas, and shook out my forearms. After the tingling stopped, I toured the caldarium.

Now I know that the voice hadn't arisen out of the dream. Hadn't been a man's even. The sixty-a-day timbre had foxed me initially, but I'm certain it belonged to a woman. Well, confident that it was more Lauren Bacall than Orson Welles. No – Not Bacall. There was no warmth in it. More Mercedes

McCambridge.

Gruesome? It sounded the way she looks. But why does she deign to talk to me only after I enter the hammam?

Daph

24 APRIL 2004, 21:25

Particulars, Universals,

Though exhausted, I didn't return to my room after dinner. Instead, I went into the bar, mounted a stool, and waited for Mercedes to give herself away.

Barman today, Shaz asked about the mother country each time we were alone: the job market, housing situation, et cetera. I obliged, answering as best I could, even after he turned to football.

Shortly after nine, it occurred to me that I had taken it for granted that Mercedes was a local. However, her timbre – basso, almost profundo – confused the issue. There had been an accent, yes, but it might have been a German one. This inspired a suspicion that it had been someone from last summer's conference.

None of my fellow guests looked familiar. Then, it needn't have been anyone I had been introduced to. Maybe it was someone who had seen me deliver my paper. That would explain Mercedes' familiarity with my title too. But the animosity? I'm used to my treatises inspiring perplexity, but offence?

Perhaps it hadn't been the paper that had annoyed – the subject matter, conclusion – but the Q and A session afterwards. I've been known to rub commentators up the wrong way (pause for knowing laughter to circle the common-room); did I do as much on that occasion? (Be honest.) I don't recall doing so. Then, that's rather the way with these things, isn't it?

To my recollection, only one woman had dared ask a question. A Nordic type, lean, pale. And she had had a high-pitched voice.

Emboldened by one pint more of all-inclusive Riesling, I levelled with Shaz. Not wishing to seem to be recalling his assault, I didn't mention where I had heard Mercedes' voice; I described it merely.

He drew in his chin, and said that there was no one like that in the hotel. Then, he dashed to the other end of the bar – though there was no one waiting on him there – and busied himself folding napkins.

Why had he behaved so peculiarly? Later, the answer came to me: it hadn't been for the usual reason, on account of the unsightly mozzie bite on the end of my nose, or because he hadn't understood what I'd said. No – The darling had been a gentleman.

A female guest with a voice that might be mistaken

for a man's? That's me to a tee!

Daph

25 APRIL 2004, 11:02

Particulars, Universals,

Today I surrendered another ten years of my life to terror.

I arose later than intended, and missed the dolmus into town. Hearing tinkling bells, I decided not to return to the hotel to await the next one. Energised by the prospect of being nuzzled by a herd of querulous mountain goats, I crossed the road, and started up the hill. After five minutes or so, I stopped looking out for rabbit holes, and glanced up.

A great silhouette gambolled over the peak, and started down the incline. A ram?

I removed my sunglasses, and opened my handbag. Before my fingers located my seeing specs, I knew what the shadowy figure had to be.

Unable to recall Jim's counsel regarding the brute we happened upon on our honeymoon, I froze. What to do: face it down or present my back to it? Certain that Cerberus would sink its fangs into my face first, I turned aside at the last second. It snapped at me, bounded past, and away.

I removed my hand from my chest, and patted the seat of my trousers. The prick of its canines, breath on my flesh – I had felt them. However, the material seemed to be intact, and my palm came away white.

The soft chimes gave way to harsh percussion. I was perplexed again. If I continued to climb – remained still, even – Cerberus was sure to believe that I had intentions on his charges, but if I started down, he might conclude that I meant to challenge him.

I descended slowly. After I rounded the last hillock, I started.

Cerberus had squatted down in the road in the manner of a Sphinx. I clutched my throat, and tiptoed towards the dolmus stop. Cerberus growled when I approached, but didn't get to his feet.

A new maxim: where there are goat herds, there will be guard dogs. Not the soppy collies we fuss over when rambling in the Cotswolds, but great, fanged killers.

Daph

26 APRIL 2004, 12:05

Particulars, Universals,

Example of an act of faith: the ascent to the mountain village of Şirince by coach.

Example of the collective will: though not a single passenger left their seat, every one played a part in preventing the vehicle from veering off each hairpin bend.

When Jim and I visited, this village was a self-sustaining community that had recently deigned to admit visitors. Now it is an unabashed tourist trap as authentic as an Epcot pavilion.

I toured it three times in pursuit of something of genuine worth. Failing, I returned to the market, and purchased a dozen bars of olive oil soap. Then, I toured the wine shacks. All offered identical arrays of irregular plonk.

Watching a German couple gargle blackberry burgundy with the earnestness of Château Margaux quality controllers, I recalled Jim doing as much. However, I don't remember him uncorking any of the novelty tipples purchased. I must go down into the cellar when I get back. Maybe pomegranate Merlot improves after having been laid down for a couple of decades.

Overcome by a coughing fit (pollen?), I crossed to a café, and ordered an apple tea. Before it arrived, a severe young man with a shaven head sat at my table, and – unmoved by my desperate efforts to respire – puffed the virtues of his jelly vinos.

After my tea arrived, and I had recovered, he started on about the Jeep safaris he ran as a sideline. Apparently, the Americans he had driven to the summit of Mount Mycale on the last one had been so rude that he had abandoned them there. Without taking a breath, he asked if I would like to accompany him on the next trip. I drained my glass, and told him that my itinerary had been determined before I had arrived.

He looked me over in a peculiar – suggestive? - manner, and started on about his wines again (superior to all the other 'piss' on offer, apparently). I purchased three bottles, as much to dismiss as indulge him. On my return, I'll leave them in the common-room – along with the soap – for you to fight over.

Daph

26 APRIL 2004, 14:59

Particulars, Universals,

Extravagance was the order of today's excursion. An air-conditioned coach picked me up outside the hotel. Only eight other tourists joined me on it. The sole Brit, I had been assigned my own guide: another Classics student. I didn't have the heart to tell him that I had German.

The journey to Pamukkale, Classics revealed, would take approximately three hours. If I didn't mind, he would impart everything else I needed to know after we arrived. I nodded. He sprawled across the bank of seats opposite, and promptly fell asleep.

The party in front – comprised of young women – were entertained throughout the journey. I couldn't make out what their guide was saying (odd how sentences in a second language have to be heard clearly and entirely to be comprehended, while ones in a first can be recreated from the odd word), but the laughter rarely dried.

I tried to stay awake, but there are only so many distant hills one's gaze can range over. And only so many glimpses of a recumbent young god one can steal. (I didn't blame him for being as entertaining as a corpse; I wasn't *mother* to him; more *grandmother*.)

I woke from the Jim dream into a coughing fit. This time, I had a bottle of water to hand. Nevertheless, I alighted from the coach spluttering and shuddering. Before outlining the history of the resort, my guide cleared his throat; so perhaps both of us had fallen victim to the air-conditioning. His English wasn't as facile as his colleague's German. Self-consciousness soon overcame him. I asked if he minded if I toured the site alone, citing sentimental reasons. Brightening, he nodded vigorously.

An image of Jim and I frolicking in a sparkling travertine flashed across my mind. Memory or imagination? In an effort to determine which, I started towards one of them. After slipping across glassy limestone, I fell backwards, bumped my head, and slid down the slope – not towards the calcium carbonate pool, but the precipice to the side of it. I glanced left and right. Nothing was in grabbing distance. The safety tape marking the cliff edge came on fast. I screamed. After the awful racket stopped, I opened my eyes. The single cloud overhead floated forward. A scrum of burly young Germans deposited me on flat ground.

Despite not having packed my swimming cosie, I

determined to cool my blushes with a dip in the pool of Hierapolis. The mineral-rich thermal spring was unsuited to the task; reminding me of nothing so much as salted pasta water at the simmer. The tadpoles darting about in it looked like trofiette. What was I, then, in me combinations? A great suet pudding stewing.

Daph

P.S.

Mufti manned the resort's apple tea concession.

27 APRIL 2004,
12:46

Particulars, Universals,

I wandered today's ruin in the company of Santa Claus' enormous family. His extended clan, that is; not a fraternity of the obese related by blood.

His eldest son – the spindly Goth – trailed far behind, chin on his chest. Clearly, this excursion – the entire holiday – was retribution for something he had done; in a past life possibly.

Though there is less of the Ancient Greek city present than absent these days, our guide acquitted himself well. Often, a single hunk of rubble marks the original location of a wall one plethron long. Nevertheless, he worked up the original splendours with words.

Noticing that the site was unbounded by fence or wall, I asked him if it was only a matter of time before an unscrupulous billionaire decided that the remaining bits of Trajaneum would make fetching garden ornaments. He looked flummoxed. Serves him right for asking *the dreaded question* when he introduced himself.

After he claimed that the base of the altar dedicated to Zeus was the throne of Satan mentioned in the Book of Revelations, we all turned towards Spindly. Or where he was last seen.

It was only after our guide moved on that I noticed cigarette smoke rising from the base of the votive tree, up through the branches bent low with evil eye medallions.

Daph

28 APRIL 2004, 15:15

Particulars, Universals,

The builders are in. A drill as raucous as the trumpets of the Apocalypse started up when I reached the check-in desk to the hammam. I clapped a hand to my heart. Gruesome didn't so much as blench. Why had the hotel employed a deaf, dumb and blind old lady to administer their baths?

Stretching out on the goebektasas, it occurred to me that she may be ill. She looked as pale as the wall behind her today. Offering her employment must have been an act of charity.

Shortly after my tellak retired, someone coughed for attention. I pushed myself off the stone, and peered about. My gaze returned to the tinkling fountain. The steam thinned to reveal a gargantuan figure installed in the stone seat – throne? – to the left of it. Mercedes? With its hair scraped back, it was impossible to tell whether it was male or female. Even the pendulous breasts didn't settle the matter, given its bulk. Maybe this had been my tellak?

Its eyelids fluttered. Deep set in the great brown head, the whites shone, bright as sodium. The steam between us thickened.

Determining to test my hunch by speaking first, I inquired after Gruesome. Drubbed by steam, my voice sounded frail and thin. I persisted; asking after Gruesome's welfare. No response. Certain that my companion hadn't heard me – couldn't have done – I cleared my throat prior to repeating myself.

I was startled by a booming cackle. The queer thing was, it didn't seem to emanate from the seat – that direction – but from everywhere, nowhere.

'Perhaps she's the ghost.'

It was Mercedes. Her voice.

She went on to tell me about the original keeper of the bathhouse, whose spirit was said to haunt it, dispensing evil airs. 'It's haram, of course.'

I prepared to counter that Turkey claimed to be a secular state. Stopped myself. Failing to come up with a less provocative formulation, I told her that I don't believe in ghosts.

'I thought you did,' she said. 'You philosophers.'

Unable to recall one thinker who had commented on the supernatural, let alone affirmed faith in same, I asked her what she had meant.

The steam jets surged. After a minute or so, I pushed myself up. Blind, I circled the goebektasas, my fingers ever in contact with the stone. A hundred and eighty degrees round it, I turned, and started towards the seat. It was nearer than anticipated. A fact I ascertained only after I stubbed the big toe on my left foot on something sharp at its base. I swore loudly.

Hearing the cackle, I turned towards the tepidarium, and called out. The frigidarium. Receiving no reply from either, I clacked to the changing room.

There was no one there.

Daph

28 APRIL 2004, 20:45

Particulars, Universals,

Dinner digested, I hobbled towards the bar to engage in another evening of Mercedes coursing.

Starting, I stopped in the doorway. What was going on?

Elderly guests – their faces pinched with concentration – lindy-hopped before a live band. Among them, Santa Claus flung a woman a third of his height and girth about him. After the music stopped, he and she bumped lips. That particular clone, then, had to be his wife.

It occurred to me that he might have been the creature in the seat. He shouldn't have been in the hammam at that time of day, of course. Then, neither should I have been when I first visited it. Perhaps his eyesight is as poor as my own.

A young man descended from the dais, and started towards me. The look on his face: revulsion? Fear?

He drew close, and asked the dreaded question. I tutted, and turned to those whooping and applauding. Undaunted, Fearful put out a hand. Determined not to be animated, I barked 'Kranken'. He nodded vigorously – with understanding or relief. I turned towards the bar.

It took aeons for Shaz to get to me. In the meantime, German after German persisted in asking *the dreaded question*. After I had downed a stein or more of Liebfraumilch, a likely reason why I, alone, inspire the query occurred to me.

It's due to the damned hammam, isn't it? Each time I visit it, I steam-clean away the melanin that rose in me the day before. At this rate, I'll return to Blighty looking paler than when I left it.

Shaz wasn't forthcoming this evening. Deciding that he was busy merely – the bar was packed – I cut to the chase: asked if he had any gen on Mercedes. He glanced about warily, and leaned towards me -

Someone shouted his name. He jumped out of his skin, and hared to the other end of the bar. Three animators buttonholed him, and whispered in urgent Turkish. He bowed his head, and nodded repeatedly.

Concerned that I had landed him in it, I hobbled across. The huddle broke up. Ignoring my entreaties, Shaz dashed towards the agora. Fearful assured me that everything was in order, and asked if I would like another glass of wine.

Daph

29 APRIL 2004, 10:45

Particulars, Universals,

I descended to reception to book an hour in the net cafe. Officious offered to call a doctor for me instead. 'What on earth for?' I said. Her gaze fell to my feet, the bandage on my toe. I assured her that I was fine. That, at my age, everything ached or bled. 'If I call a quack every time I get a knock or bruise, I'll bankrupt the NHS.' She didn't laugh.

Instead, she offered to fetch me a wheelchair. I demurred, but settled for the walking stick she drew out from under her desk – to stop her fussing – and joked that it might make me look distinguished. Given the expressions on the faces of the fellow tourists I passed on my way to the net cafe, I suspect that it made me look like an old crone. More like one.

I powered up my allotted PC determined to discover what Mercedes had meant about us philosophers. Perhaps she had misunderstood the point of Ryle's *ghost in the machine*? Or Hegel's *Phenomenology of*

Spirit? However, after I entered the word *ghost* in the search engine, it returned national, regional, and parochial matches first – dragging me down an altogether different rabbit hole.

It turns out that our hammam is haunted. Or purported to be. Something to do with an old story about an attendant of death that pre-dates the Muslim religion. Goes all the way back to Ishtar, the queen of hell:

'Let her dwell here with heroes who have left their wives,
Wives who have left the embrace of their husbands,
With luckless children who have perished before their time.
Go, porter, open to her thy gate.
Make an end with her as with former visitors.'

Daph

30 APRIL 2004, 11:47

Particulars, Universals,

This time, the dream was set at night, in total darkness, save for the illuminated water.

Why hadn't I joined Jim in the pool? After all, night swimming is regarded as romantic. It might have been, had the pool been heated. How could I tell that it hadn't been? At first, I had suspected that the mist rolling across the water was steam. Then, I spotted something under it, across the entire surface: ice; a solid sheet of ice. And in the centre of it, Jim, smiling and gesturing: come on in!

I started awake with my head throbbing. Noticing scarlet spots on my pillow, I feared that I had fallen asleep in my pancake again. But the dresser mirror said no. I drew my brush through my hair, and yelped with pain. On fingering my scalp, I compassed a scab the size of a golf ball; just when I had put my headaches down to the cleaning fluids used here.

I unravelled the dressing from my toe – no worse but no better – and cleaned and redressed the wound. Determined to get to the bottom of the philosophy of the supernatural, I descended to the net cafe, and self-quarantined with one pitta and a bottle of water.

Trawling through the online *Encyclopedia of Philosophy*, I was unable to locate a single treatise on ghosts, ancient or modern. Other than for theists, the supernatural had metaphorical value only. True, a *ghost club* had been established in the other place, but that had concerned itself with debunking, not affirming.

True, William James had founded the *American Society For Psychical Research*. But it can't have been a mere coincidence that he had done so shortly after the death of his son. Moreover, like Freud, he had seemed to be interested in the supernatural more as a psychological than ontological phenomenon.

Why had Mercedes claimed otherwise? You're probably all ahead of me on this -

Then I remembered that the last conference had been entitled *Ghosts*. So, Mercedes – or someone she/he knows – must have been in attendance after all.

Nevertheless, having no desire to do anything else, I persevered. (Who knows, I may get a paper out of this.) Pursuing ontology (the dirt tracks of being and nothingness, being and time), the junction of mind-matter, I pushed through until I reached the identity of indiscernibles.

Had Leibniz touched on the supernatural? Tim knows the answer to that. However, the supreme rationalist had insisted that two objects occupying the same spacetime must, of necessity, be the same thing.

All right, but what might he have dubbed the same object occupying different spacetimes?

Daph

30 APRIL 2004, 16:45

Woke in a muck sweat, head and foot pounding, but with everything worked out. Wrote it down. All of it. As it came to me. I'll pretty it up later.

Exhilarated by my discoveries, I descended to the hammam as soon as it opened to put them to Mercedes. I took my specs with me this time. Not dawdling at the check-in desk, I didn't stop until I reached the sıcaklık. Why wasn't there any steam? Or anyone about? I hobbled through the other two chambers. They were empty, too.

Determined to get something out of Gruesome at last, I returned to the check-in desk. She wasn't on duty, but someone was skulking behind it – bent, pale. I slipped on my glasses, and started. When had a mirror been affixed to the back wall?

Hearing voices, I turned. Two builders limped towards me, hauling scaffolding equipment. I approached them, and asked after Gruesome. They regarded me uncertainly. I repeated my query in

German. They turned to one another, and whispered in Turkish. The shorter one set his poles against the check-in desk, and said, 'No check-in lady.'

'No -' I said. 'Not now. Earlier. Yesterday.'

He continued to watch me – my lips – after I finished, as if expecting more. Then, he said, 'Close for work', and moved his hands in front of one another quickly, to signal cease and desist.

I asked about the mirror. Shorty didn't disguise his impatience. 'Always been there,' he said. 'Since hotel started.'

After he turned away, something else occurred to me. I shouted. Shorty jumped out of his skin. I raised my complimentary pass. He regarded it mistrustfully. I held it out to him. He accepted it gingerly; his right thumb and index finger gripping one edge only, as if the cardboard were contaminated. He screwed his eyes, muttered, frowned. Then, the scales fell.

'Other one,' he said.

'Other what?' I asked.

'Other hammam,' he said.

The hotel had two hammams?

'Other hotel,' he said. 'This one closed for fix.'

'Since when?' I said.

He counted on his fingers. 'Six – eight week.'

Why was he lying?

56

01 MAY 2004, 03:18

Understand all now.

Who Gruesome was.

What ailed her.

Saw her when I sat down to type this.

See her now.

In the dressing table mirror.

Beside Mufti.

14 MAY 2004, 10:03

Florence,

Following your telephone call of 13 May, please find, attached:

(a) 22 e-mails that your aunt sent to us prior to her fall,

(b) 2 unsent e-mails discovered in the *drafts* folder of her Blackberry after it,

(c) a JPG of her foolscap notes,

(d) a Word document offering a partial transcription of same.

To expand on my spoken comments regarding the notes:

Form:

Daphne was justly proud of her copperplate; the cursive on the page of foolscap is almost illegible. Consequently, at first, we were uncertain that she was the author, or which language the notes had been written in. Presumably, your aunt jotted them down in a race against her worsening condition.

Her former secretary, Joyce Allsop, came out of retirement to transcribe them. After a great deal of effort, she succeeded in deciphering a third of the text. I'm afraid we must await a Champollion of handwriting to decrypt the remainder.

Content:

Though Daphne was a playful correspondent, she was a supremely logical thinker. So, we can only conclude that she experienced a mental breakdown in the final stages of the illness that took her from us.

I feel I ought to elaborate on my remark dismissing the supernatural:

I remain a disbeliever. Regards the paranormal, however, I am an agnostic. I know many people who claim to have experienced the uncanny. Upright citizens who had no ulterior motive for so doing; my own grandmother, for one. My conclusion? There may be more things in heaven and earth than are dreamt of in our philosophy, but there are definitely more things in head and heart that are known to our psychology.

Yours,

Tim Cavendish

P.S.

Your aunt's belongings were forwarded from the Mati hotel to the İzmir hospital, and from the hospital to us after her demise. Would you like me to send them to you?

TRANSCRIPTION (PARTIAL)

No such things as ghosts.

What appears as disembodied spirit is [a] projection from [a] creature of substance out of phase in [the] space-time continuum.

[It is] possible that I am – even now – appearing as a phantom in another dimension.

In this other-verse, identical to ours in every particular, [a] sudden rip/surge in energy presents matter at a fraction of its original strength, dimensionless, as outline only.

To balance this, [the] original subject experiences a drain on its [elan vital?].

A spasm of overwhelming weakness that occasions [a] heart attack/seizure.

Conservation of energy is maintained across multiverses.

For an additional spurt to accrue in one, another must yield [an] equal gobbet of energy.

[I have] yet to formulate [a] logical reason for this anomaly.

Need there be one?

[It is] more surprising – given [the] circumstances necessary to create/sustain existence – that glitches do not occur more often.

Genuine paranormal events – experienced by witnesses beyond reproach – invariably bring on feelings of intense weakness/cold/heat before/after [the] incident.

Leibniz reasoned [that] two objects occupying the same spacetime must, of necessity, be the same thing.

This is [a] case of an object not occupying the same spacetime.

Occupying the same space at different times.

Out of kilter with its timeline.

Conversely, [a] subject might haunt itself.

Be projected into [its] own past.

Appear as [a] ghost from [its] own future.

Could be [a] future natural law.

What are the natural forces?

Why do things behave as they do?

What governs that they must?

Ensures this behaviour is [permitted?] and not that?

Not god, but a godlike determinant.

Science or philosophy?

With M and string theory, is there any difference now?

Science = philosophy with toys.

Not a solution that pleases a philosopher merely, but [a] philosophical solution.

After Aristotle, metaphysics is that which [is] after physics.

This [is] meta-philosophy.

Once, all learning was dubbed philosophy.

Then, it evolved/devolved.

Split/spilled into branches/tranches.

First, [ethics?], politics, natural science.

Then, on the last strand, physics, chemistry, biology.

The former split into [?] and [?].

Now, quantum physics is [a] field of its own with

[as] many subdivisions as the whole of natural philosophy once had [boasted].

Similarly, [the] history of the universe has been particularised/dissected.

Particle, cell, atom, nucleus, [gluon?], quark.

Forces, too, have evolved.

Gravity, electricity, weak, dark matter, relativity, [steady state?].

In [the] endless bifurcation of certainty/doubt, there is a place for random generation.

For [a] fully-formed chicken to bypass evolution – egg – to appear spontaneously, feathered, clucking.

ABOUT THE AUTHOR

Richard Morley

Richard Morley is the author of the blog:

https://suspicionsandsuperstitions.com

and creator/programmer of the writing app:

little acorns